成寒英語有聲書 ③

尼斯湖水怪
之謎

成 寒◎編著

The Mystery
of the
Loch Ness Monster

目　錄

目　錄

尼斯湖水怪之謎有聲故事內文

知識性、故事性、趣味性的英語有聲書

這部《尼斯湖水怪之謎》
是實地報導的英語有聲書，
音質清晰，如歷現場。一共有
２１段，文體全部以「現在式」
（present tense）書寫，句型結構簡單。

如
何
使
用
本
書

學習方法：
請參閱成寒著《英文，非學好不可》
及《早早開始，慢慢來》兩本書。

〔推薦序〕

悦聽與泛聽

◎金　堅

　　我覺得成寒《躺著學英文》這個書名取得不但富創意，更是一語道出學英文的祕訣。學英文不必正襟危坐，掙扎苦讀，大可輕輕鬆鬆，以愉悅的心情，享受學習的樂趣。一旦有了樂趣，就會有學習動機；有了動機，自然會主動廣泛接觸，英文能力也在不知不覺中跟著提升，這是一種良性的循環。

　　成寒以個人成功的學習經驗，提供教室以外學習英文的途徑及資源，正好彌補台灣學生學英文的最大缺憾：聽得太少。由於聽的不足，不但會影響說英文時的語調、發音，對讀、寫的流利、用字等方面也造成極大的困難。

　　成寒【英語有聲書系列】內有情境式有聲故事，「正常速度」的真實英文，以精采的情節引人入勝，也符合了全語言教學的理念。「正常速度」的英文對許多人來說是難以適應的，因為聽慣教學錄音帶中刻意放慢速度的「教室英文」，一旦與外國人交談時，耳朵不習慣真實英文，以致雞同鴨講，專研多年的文法完全無用武之地。成寒【英語有聲書系列】是帶領有心學好英文的人，走向「悅聽」（pleasure listening）與「泛聽」（extensive listening）的橋樑，Why not give it a try?

雖然今天台灣的英語教育逐漸轉變，但是仍存在一些隱憂。以下是我對台灣英語教育的感想及呼籲，謹供大家參考：

第一、由於傳統英文教學太重視「精讀」，使得學生的精力集中在鑽研文法、拼字正確。一篇文章被肢解得支離破碎，只剩下脫離上下文的英文單字學習。學生不但依然常翻字典，也依賴老師冗長的解說、分析，一字一句講解讀本，力求逐字逐句翻譯的完全理解，缺乏掌握重點的訓練，以致學生見樹不見林。其實聽、說、讀的學習策略是相通的，均得運用預知、猜測、推敲、推論等技巧，教師須鼓勵學生不必聽懂、看懂每一個字，只要藉關鍵字，掌握文意即可。

第二、過度「精讀」的結果，會導致忽略「悅聽」、「悅讀」與「泛聽」、「泛讀」的重要性。由於時間過分花費在精讀方面，以致甚少涉獵課外讀物；美國兒童、青少年從小大量閱讀有趣、適合其年齡層的讀本或故事書。看得多、聽得多，在無形中累積英文的素養。台灣學生卻跳過這個「語法自然流利、用字正確」的訓練階段，直接研讀學科英文，以致造成極大的鴻溝。

第三、自從全民英檢測驗開始，市面上充斥英檢題目供學生練習，但有些學生本末倒置，只讀考題而很少讀真正的英文，只靠答題技巧熟練而拿高分，如此對英文能力的加強實在有限。長久考試引導教學，導致學生被動、偏差的學習態度，變成只求提高英檢成績，不求提升自己英語程度。一旦考試的壓力消失，就從此遠離英文。

「廣泛的聽、讀」與「愉悅的聽、讀」一直是台灣英語教育長久缺乏的。不論是哪一方面，都應該以學生的興趣及分級程度為主，主題包羅萬象如科幻、電影、文藝、體育、傳記、名著改寫、動物、懸疑小說、童話、社會、商業等。每本可由幾百個單字到幾千個單字，由淺而深，循序漸進，以訓練流利度為主。學生在不須查字典之下就能猜懂七、八成為適合程度前提。

盼各級學校重視「悅讀」、「悅聽」與「泛讀」、「泛聽」，而不是抱著一本教科書死啃，以致課外讀物成為遙不可及的補充教材。圖書館大量採購有聲課外讀物，以彌補學生平常聽到少之又少的英文，帶動聽、讀風氣。教師重新調整教學目標、課程及考試題型，讓學生多聽、多讀自己有興趣的書報雜誌，好好享受閱讀及聽英文的樂趣。

（本文作者為東吳大學英文系副教授）

WELCOME TO

THE ORIGINAL

LOCH NESS

MONSTER

VISITOR CENTRE

CAR PARK & HOTEL →

>>> COACH PARKING >>>

〔前言〕

遇見水怪？

成　寒

"Really?"（真的嗎？）

那一年夏天我從英國旅行歸來，回到美國大學上課。中午，一如往常在學校餐廳裡用餐時，興致盎然地向同桌聯合國食友宣稱我這回在蘇格蘭遇見尼斯湖水怪。眾人聽了，莫

▶ 蘇格蘭鄉間，綠草綿延覆蓋著起伏的山丘，羊群像星星點點。（成寒　攝）

不睜大了眼睛，露出不可置信的表情！

　　不騙你們，我真的看見水怪！好大一隻。

　　記得我是從倫敦搭上夜火車，睡臥鋪，匡郎匡郎匡郎，一覺醒來已是蘇格蘭首府愛丁堡。清晨，風微涼。次日午後轉乘巴士，穿過鄉間，田野一片連著一片，綠草綿延覆蓋著起伏的山丘，田野中或白或黑，像星星點點，那是羊群。來到因佛尼斯已是黃昏時分，我一個人漫步在尼斯湖畔，遇到四個年輕的蘇格蘭衛兵，他們的制服居然是短裙，我努力忍住不笑出聲來。

年輕的蘇格蘭衛兵，穿短裙制服。
（成寒 攝）

蘇格蘭以威士忌聞名,這一望便知
是釀酒廠。(成寒 攝)

　　這會兒,一個不小心,我腳下差點兒踩到一隻身子很
長、模樣怪異、形狀醜陋,爬行緩慢的怪物,當場嚇得幾乎
要尖叫出聲。結果牠也被我嚇了一跳,忙不迭地,撲通一聲
跳入尼斯湖裡,激起幾圈漣漪,轉眼間消失蹤影。

　　尼斯湖水怪,名氣實在有夠大!我很小的時候就已經聽
說,只是一直不知道是真是假。

　　我在因佛尼斯住的 B & B(註),由一對老夫婦主持,兒
女長大以後,他們把空出的兩個房間作民宿。我看那房子越
看越有趣,屋頂上煙囪羅列。問老先生,幹嘛要弄那麼多根
煙囪?

　　他向我解釋：「一根煙囪代表一個房間；有多少個房間，就有多少根煙囪。」

　　老先生臉上爬滿皺紋，人很和氣。晚餐，喝下一杯蘇格蘭威士，他興致來了，娓娓道起這些年來親眼目睹水怪有五次之多。一次是在清晨時分，他剛好開車經過湖邊，驀然間，看見一隻龐然大物悄然從湖中升起，濺起一連串的水花和泡沫。

　　老先生相信，尼斯湖深水底下一定有水怪，而且不只一隻。

一根煙囪代表一個房間；有多少根
煙囪，就有多少個房間。（成寒 攝）

　　多年來，尼斯湖水怪一向被斥為無稽之談，當地民眾不知聽過多少遍，每個人都把它當作民間傳說，一笑置之。

　　但自從英國人提姆‧丁斯岱爾（Tim Dinsdale, 1924-1987）拍攝的影片在電視上放映，觀眾親眼看到半身沒在水面下的巨大動物的背部，赤褐色的峰背形體，緩緩地成之字形游開，消失在水面下。這時候，以前見過「水怪」的人紛紛提出他們的見證。

　　──像天鵝式的長脖子，上面頂著有如爬蟲類的扁平腦袋瓜，露出水面六呎，後面拖著足足有三十呎長，起伏如駝峰的黝黑身體。

　　──在水面上，三個駝峰起伏，留下一條冒泡的水痕。頭和頸一樣寬，嘴寬十二吋至十八吋；遠望如象背，四呎高，十二呎長。游過後水痕如同魚雷的水痕，速度約每小時三十五哩。

　　──好像一隻大海參！

　　──似乎很怕噪音，一聽到汽船的馬達聲立刻潛匿水底，不再現身。

這是真的水怪嗎？

從那時起，一群博物學家組成的尼斯湖水怪調查團開始展開行動。一九六四年，他們把丁斯岱爾的影片交給專家檢驗，把原片放大二十倍，一寸一寸分析，報告結果指出：浮出水線的物體以時速十哩的速度移動，應該不是船隻或潛水艇，可能是一個有生命的物體。從牠露出水面的軀體推斷，這個物體的橫斷面至少有六呎寬，五呎高。

在湖面作觀察時，他們在這長條形湖泊的一端裝置雷達設備，加上紅外線攝影，可以拍攝常在夜間出沒的水怪。水下追蹤時，他們利用「聲納」（sonar），也就是有聲書內文裡的「特製錄音機」（special tape recorders）。

根據目前公開的照片及一百多位目擊者的報告，有人畫出這個神祕巨獸的模樣，且製作出模型。的確，牠是一種奇形怪狀的動物。有人認為牠像古代的蛇頸龍——恐龍時代一

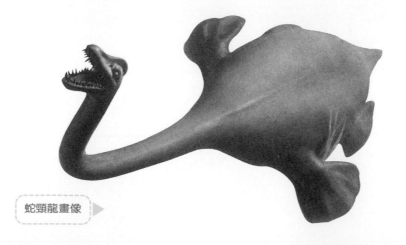

蛇頸龍畫像 ▶

種吃魚、產卵的爬蟲類，七千萬年前已經絕種。這種巨獸適於在大海中生存，體長達三十呎。牠的軀體像大木桶，四肢像划槳，頸部細長，頭小，大嘴巴，牙齒尖銳。

在尼斯湖發現這種活生物，倘若是真的，這無疑將是一大轟動事件。雖然有人不相信，但也不無可能。例如史前時代的一種「腔棘魚」（coelacanth），人們一直認為已在七千萬年前絕跡，然而一九三八年卻在非洲海岸外捕到這樣一條活魚。

然而，到底水怪是如何游進尼斯湖裡的呢？

許多人都認為是從海裡游過來的。在冰河時期以前，尼斯湖是與海相連的海灣。後來冰融化，地殼上升，尼斯湖便成為四面環陸的淡水內陸湖。

空棘魚是史前時代的生物，本來已經絕種，沒想到二十世紀又出現其蹤跡。

今天，尼斯湖的湖面高出海平面約五十二呎。湖水永不結冰，常年水溫幾乎維持不變。湖長約三十八點六公里，湖寬約一點六公里，是歐洲最深的湖泊之一。湖水最深處達兩百九十公尺深。平坦的泥湖底溫度經常維持攝氏六度，水裡有重達三十磅的鮭魚、十五磅至二十磅的鱒魚和梭子魚。這種環境正適合行蹤詭祕的水怪藏身之處。

聽完我的旅行敘說，大家覺得意猶未盡，各種問題此起彼落。誰知在座有個金髮老美很掃興，居然直言說我在尼斯湖畔看見的，哪是什麼水怪，不過是一隻體形較大的蛞蝓（slug），或是海豹（seal）、蜥蜴（lizard）罷了。如此大驚小怪，真是沒見識！

＊　　　＊　　　＊　　　＊　　　＊　　　＊

相關報導

根據二〇〇三年七月新聞報導：

有人在尼斯湖淺水中發現一具一億五千萬年前的長頸、肉食海洋爬蟲生物化石遺骸。這四塊保存完好的蛇頸龍脊椎骨嵌在石灰石中，表面看得見脊椎和血管。眾人相信，這塊化石表示水怪之類的生物當年曾經在尼斯湖活動。

＊　　　＊　　　＊　　　＊　　　＊　　　＊

根據二〇〇三年七月新聞報導：

專家利用六百個聲納電波與衛星導航技術搜尋尼斯湖，

並未發現傳說中尼斯湖水怪的蹤跡。

　　搜尋小組認為，儘管一般的水中爬蟲類動物大多活躍於亞熱帶地區，尼斯湖的寒冷湖水可能也適合恐龍時代的蛇頸龍生存。然而到處搜尋，幾乎搜遍整個尼斯湖，就是找不到湖中有大型生物活動的跡象。

　　搜尋小組指出，尼斯湖水怪的傳聞歷久不衰，唯一合理的解釋是，人們看到他們想要看的幻覺。為了證明他們的說法，小組在湖面下暗藏一根籬笆柱，並在一群遊客面前慢慢升起，事後有人就畫出類似水怪頭部的圖形。

　　＊　　　＊　　　＊　　　＊　　　＊　　　＊

　　根據二○○三年十月新聞報導：

　　四十一歲的英國人史考特穿著老式笨重的潛水衣，戴著十八公斤重的金屬頭盔，在尼斯湖底步行四十一點六公里，長達十二天，目的是為了替白血病童募款。途中，腳下有時踩的是爛泥，有時是石塊或什麼都不是。但他說一路上都沒有見到水怪。

註：B ＆ B：Bed and Breakfast，英國盛行的民宿，供應早餐。

＊有關英文學習上的問題，請上成寒網站：www.chenhen.com

尼斯湖水怪之謎

The mystery of Loch Ness

CD * 1

The **Loch** Ness **Monster**.

A **famous** monster.

A famous mystery.

Yes, the Loch Ness Monster is a **mystery**.

People ask, "What is in Loch Ness?"

"Is it a monster?"

"Is the Loch Ness Monster real?"

People ask those questions, but they don't know the answers. That is the mystery—the mystery of Loch Ness.

This book tells the **story** of that mystery. It tells the real story of the Loch Ness Monster.

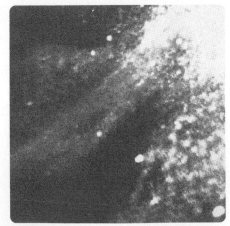

一團黝黑的陰影——
這是尼斯湖水怪嗎？

尼斯湖之謎

CD＊1

尼斯湖水怪。

一隻著名的水怪。

一個著名的謎。

是的，尼斯湖水怪是個謎。

有人問：「尼斯湖裡到底是什麼東西？」

「是一隻水怪嗎？」

「尼斯湖水怪是真的嗎？」

人們提出那些問題，可是他們不知道答案。那就是謎──尼斯湖之謎。

這本書訴說那個謎的報導，訴說有關尼斯湖水怪的真實報導。

loch (*n.*)
湖（參看P.24.
25的解釋）

monster (*n.*)
怪物

famous (*adj.*)
著名的

mystery (*n.*)
謎、神祕、
神祕的事物

story (*n.*)
故事、報導

這張著名的「外科醫生的水怪照片」，經電腦分析後，證明是假的。

What is a monster?

CD ＊ 2

What is a monster?

It's a big animal or a big fish. It's big and it's **strange**. A small animal or fish can be strange, too. But we don't say, "that's a monster."

A monster is always big.

怪物的定義？

CD ＊ 2

怪物是什麼？

是一隻大的動物或大條魚，體積大，長相怪異。小動物或魚也有很奇怪的，但我們不說那是「怪物」。

怪物永遠都是大的。

strange (*adj.*)
奇怪的、怪異的

What is a loch?

CD * 3

It's a strange word, "loch". It is a **Scottish** word. **English** people say "lake". Scottish people say "loch". A "loch" is a kind of lake in Scotland, a lake between two **hills**.

Loch Ness is not the only loch in Scotland, but it is a famous loch. Loch Ness is not the only loch with a monster, but the Loch Ness Monster is the famous monster.

湖的定義？

CD * 3

　　「湖」（loch）是個奇怪的字，這是蘇格蘭文。「湖」，英格蘭人說 "lake"，蘇格蘭人叫 "loch"。"loch" 是蘇格蘭地區，夾在兩座山丘之間的湖。

　　尼斯湖不是蘇格蘭唯一的湖，卻是一座著名的湖。尼斯湖不是唯一擁有水怪的湖，但尼斯湖水怪卻是知名的水怪。

Scottish (*adj.*)
蘇格蘭的

English (*adj.*)
英格蘭的

hill (*n.*)
山丘

◀◀◀ 尼斯湖位於兩座山丘之間，因水怪而蒙上一層神祕的面紗。（成寒／攝）

Scotland

CD＊4

Loch Ness is in northern **Scotland** and Scotland is part of the **United Kingdom**.

People often **speak of** Great Britain. **Great Britain** is only **England**, **Wales** and Scotland. The United Kingdom is Great Britain and **Northern Ireland**.

> 從地圖上可看出，大不列顛包括英格蘭、蘇格蘭及威爾斯，而因佛尼斯位於蘇格蘭北邊。

蘇格蘭

CD * 4

尼斯湖位於蘇格蘭北邊，而蘇格蘭是「英國」的一部分。

人們經常說到「大不列顛」，而大不列顛只包括英格蘭、威爾斯和蘇格蘭，「英國」則包括大不列顛及北愛爾蘭在內。

Scotland (*n.*)
蘇格蘭

United Kingdom
聯合王國，英國
（正式名稱 the United Kingdom of Great Britain and Northern Ireland：大不列顛及北愛爾蘭聯合王國）

speak of
說到、提及

Great Britain
（*n.*）大不列顛

England (*n.*)
英格蘭

Wales：(*n.*)
威爾斯

Northern Ireland
北愛爾蘭

You can see a **Scotsman**. He is wearing a **kilt** and playing the **bagpipes**. Men and women wear the kilt. It is part of **highland** dress. The bagpipes are also Scottish. Scotsmen in the Highlands do not always wear kilts. They do not all play bagpipes. But Scottish people are always Scottish, not English.

Say to a Scotsman, "You're Scottish," and he's your friend.

Say, "you're English, " and he's not a happy man.

穿花格短裙的蘇格蘭男子，在尼斯湖邊表演吹風笛。（成寒 攝）

你可以看到圖中的蘇格蘭男子，他穿花格短裙，吹奏風笛。男男女女都穿花格短裙，那是高地的一種服飾。風笛也是蘇格蘭的傳統。高地的蘇格蘭男子不一定穿花格短裙，他們也不是個個都會吹風笛。但是蘇格蘭人永遠是蘇格蘭人，不是英格蘭人。

倘若你對蘇格蘭人說：「你是蘇格蘭人。」他就會成為你的朋友。

若說：「你是英格蘭人。」他就會不高興。

Scotsman (*n.*) 蘇格蘭人（單數）

kilt (*n.*) 蘇格蘭花格短裙

bagpipes (*n.pl.*)蘇格蘭風笛

highland (*n.*) 高地：此處指蘇格蘭高地。

蘇格蘭男人穿傳統花格短裙，一路吹風笛走過。（成寒 攝）

Mystery of the Loch Ness Monster

Loch Ness

CD＊5

"Loch Ness is an old lake," **scientists** tell us.

Old? Yes, 25,000 years is old. It is also a long lake. It is 38.6 kilometers (24 miles) long, but only 1.6 **kilometers** (1 mile) across. Eight rivers and 228 streams run into it. The rivers and streams, small rivers, come down from the hills and the water runs into the Loch.

Loch Ness is also a deep lake, 296 **meters** (975 **feet**) deep. The water in the Loch isn't clear. You can see into clear water, but Loch Ness has only one meter of clear water.

What is under that? What is in the deep water of the Loch? That is the mystery of Loch Ness.

(please see the map of Loch Ness on P.32)

尼斯湖

CD＊5

「尼斯湖是一座古老的湖。」科學家告訴我們。

古老？是的，兩萬五千年當然是古老。尼斯湖也是一長條形的湖，湖長三十八點六公里（二十四哩），湖寬卻只有一點六公里（一哩）。有八條河及兩百二十八道溪流入湖裡。河與溪（小河）從山丘流下，注入湖裡。

尼斯湖也是一座深水湖，兩百九十六公尺深，相當於九百七十五呎。尼斯湖的水並不清澈。若是清澈的水，你可以看到湖裡面，可是尼斯湖的清澈程度只有一公尺深。

這下面是什麼？在湖的深水底下到底是什麼？那就是尼斯湖之謎。

（請參看P.32的尼斯湖地圖）

scientist (*n.*)
科學家

kilometer
(*n.*)公里

meter (*n.*)
公尺

feet (*n.*)
呎、英尺
（foot 的複數）

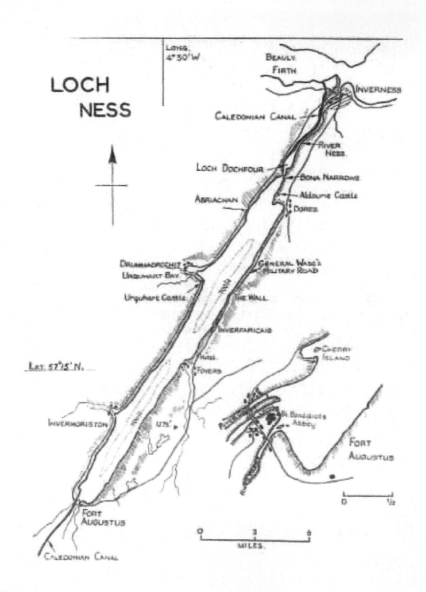

尼斯湖是一長條形的湖。

尼斯湖底下到底是什麼？那就
是尼斯湖之謎。（吳家恆攝）

Nessie

CD * 6

The Loch Ness Monster has a name. The monster is in Loch Ness, and the name of the monster is Nessie. Nessie is a real Scottish name and it is not only the name of the monster. Nessie comes from the name Agnes. Agnes—Nessie. Scottish people like the name Agnes and it is **common** in Scotland. Nessie is common, too.

The name of Loch Ness comes from the River Ness. It **runs** from Loch Ness to the town of Inverness. Inverness is **mouth** of the River Ness.

尼西

CD＊6

尼斯湖水怪有個名字，因為水怪在尼斯湖裡，所以水怪的名字就叫做「尼西」。尼西不只是水怪的名字，那是真正蘇格蘭人的名字。尼西這個名字來自艾格尼斯，艾格尼斯——尼西。蘇格蘭人喜歡艾格尼斯，這個名字在蘇格蘭是很常見的，尼西這個名字也很普遍。

尼斯湖這個名字來自尼斯河。尼斯河從尼斯湖流入因佛尼斯鎮，而因佛尼斯位於尼斯河的河口。

common (*adj.*)
普及的、普遍的、常見的

run (*v.*)
流

mouth (*n.*)
河口

秋收後，乾稻草堆捲成一團，分布於蘇格蘭田野間。（成寒 攝）

The Inverness Courier

CD * 7

The Inverness **Courier** is the name of a newspaper. The people of Inverness read it. One day, in the year 1933, they see a **headline** in the newspaper:

"Strange **spectacle** on Loch Ness! What is it?"

Under this headline is a strange story. "Man and woman see a big creature in the loch." it says. "Does a monster live in Loch Ness?"

"The monster story is not new," the newspaper says. "It's an old story, but is it a true story?"

"Yes," people say, "it's true."

People write to the newspaper. They **agree with** the story. Soon a letter comes from a Mr. Spicer. Mr. and Mrs. Spicer live in London but they often go to Scotland. One day, they are in their car near Loch Ness and they see the monster. Mr. Spicer's letter tells the story. He agrees with the newspaper.

史派瑟筆下所畫的奇怪生物。

"Yes, "Mr. Spicer writes. "The monster is there. A strange creature lives in Loch Ness. It's a **dragon**."

因佛尼斯快報

CD＊7

　　《因佛尼斯快報》是一家報紙的名稱，讀者對象是因佛尼斯鎮民。一九三三年的某一天，他們看到報紙頭條寫著：

　　「尼斯湖上不尋常的奇觀！那是什麼？」

　　頭條新聞底下是一則奇怪的報導。「衆人看見湖裡有一隻大型生物，」新聞寫道：

　　「尼斯湖裡住著一隻水怪？」

　　「水怪的故事並非第一次，」新聞寫道：「這是流傳已久的軼聞，但是真的嗎？」

　　「是的，」人們說：「是真的。」

　　人們寫信到報社，他們都贊同這個報導。不久，史派瑟先生寫來一封信。史派瑟夫婦住在倫敦，但他們經常到蘇格蘭。有一天開車經過尼斯湖附近，他們看見了水怪。史派瑟信中道出這件事，他附和報社的說法。

　　「是的，」史派瑟寫道：「的確有水怪，一隻奇怪的生物住在尼斯湖裡，那是一條龍。」

courier (*n.*)
（傳遞快信或重要文件、包裹的）信使、信差；常用作報紙名，稱作信使報或快報。

headline (*n.*)
頭條、大標題

spectacle (*n.*)
奇觀

creature (*n.*)
生物

agree with
同意、贊同

dragon (*n.*)
龍

The Daily Mail

CD * 8

The Daily Mail is a newspaper, too. It's a big and **important** London newspaper.

The **editor** of The Daily Mail sees the letter in the Inverness Courier.

"Strange creature in Loch Ness." he reads. "a dragon lives in the Loch." The editor speaks to a **reporter**, Percy Cater.

"This is a good story," he says. "An important story. But is it a true story? Go to Scotland. Speak to these people."

The Daily Mail is going to tell the story of the Loch Ness Monster.

每日郵報

CD＊8

　　《每日郵報》也是一家報紙的名稱，這是倫敦一家重要的大報。

　　《每日郵報》的編輯讀到刊登在《因佛尼斯快報》的那封信。

　　「尼斯湖裡有奇怪的生物，」他讀著：「湖裡住著一條龍。」編輯找記者柏西·卡特談話。

　　「這是一則不錯的報導，」他說：「一則重要的報導。但是真的嗎？你去蘇格蘭，找當地人談談。」

　　《每日郵報》將要作尼斯湖水怪的報導。

important (*adj.*)
重要的

editor (*n.*)
編輯

reporter (*n.*)
記者

倫敦外科醫生威爾森拍的這張水怪照片，軀體像大木桶，四肢像划槳，頸部細長，頭小，嘴大，後經電腦驗證，發現是假的。（Robert K. Wilson 攝）

Different stories

CD＊9

The Daily Mail reporter is happy. He goes to Scotland and asks **questions**. People tell him **different** things.

A man says, "The monster has a long **neck** and a big head."

But a woman says, "No, it has a short neck and a small head."

"It has two **humps**," one man tells the reporter.

"The monster has three humps," a different man says.

"Do you have your story? "The editor of The Daily Mail asks Percy Cater.

"I have different stories," the reporter says. "The monster has a short neck and a long neck, a big head and a small head. It has two or three humps."

"It's a strange monster. That's true."

不同的說法

CD＊9

　　《每日郵報》的記者很開心，他到蘇格蘭詢問當地人，大家告訴他不同的答案。

　　一個男子說：「水怪有長長的脖子和大大的頭。」

　　一個婦人卻說：「不對，牠有短短的脖子和小小的頭。」

　　「牠有兩座駝峰。」一名男子告訴記者。

　　「水怪有三座駝峰。」另一個男子說。

　　「你採訪到報導了嗎？」《每日郵報》的編輯問柏西·卡特。

　　「我有不同的報導，」記者說：「水怪有短短的脖子和長長的脖子，有大大的頭和小小的頭。牠有兩座或三座駝峰。」

　　「可以肯定的是，那是一隻奇怪的怪物。」

question (n.)
問題

different (adj.)
不同的

neck (n.)
脖子

hump (n.)
隆起的背、駝峰

◀ 水怪有三座駝峰。（Lachlan Stuart 攝）

A picture of the monster

CD * 10

Percy Cater writes stories in The Daily Mail. In one story, he says, "the creature in the Loch is a **seal**. It's not a monster."

But people say, "No, the creature cannot be a seal."

"The monster is a **whale**," Percy Cater writes in a news story.

"**Naw**, it cannot be a whale," people tell him.

In 1934, a different man, Mr. John McClean sees the creature in the Loch. Mr. McClean can **draw** and he draws a picture of the monster. It is not a seal or a whale. Soon, the **front page** of The Daily Mail has Mr. McClean's picture and the headline:

"Monster in the Loch! Mystery of Loch Ness!"

Nessie, the Loch Ness Monster is famous!

水怪圖像

CD ＊ 10

柏西・卡特在《每日郵報》寫了幾篇報導，其中一則他寫道：「湖裡的生物是海豹，不是水怪。」

可是有人說：「不對，湖裡的生物不可能是海豹。」

「水怪是一條鯨魚。」柏西・卡特另寫一則新聞報導。

「不對，那不可能是一條鯨魚。」有人告訴他。

一九三四年，另一個男子約翰・麥克連先生看到湖裡的生物。麥克連先生會畫畫，他畫了一張水怪圖像，既不像海豹也不像鯨魚。《每日郵報》頭版很快刊出麥克連的圖片作為頭條新聞：

「湖中水怪！尼斯湖之謎！」

尼西，尼斯湖水怪成名了！

◀◀◀ 水怪像一條鯨魚？（T. Crabtree 攝）

seal (*n.*)
海豹

whale (*n.*)
鯨魚

naw (*adv.*)
不，不對
（=no，但比no
語氣更強烈）

draw (*v.*)
畫、畫圖畫

front page
（報紙的）頭版

A photograph of the monster

CD＊11

Now people say, "We want a **photograph** of the Loch Ness Monster. Is it a fish, a strange creature, a dragon? What is it?"

Only a photograph can answer that question. "We want a photograph of Nessie."

The editors of newspapers agree with the people. "A photograph is important," they tell the reporters.

"Get a photograph of the monster."

Not only the newspaper reporters want a photograph of Nessie. **Visitors** come to Loch Ness from England, Wales and Ireland. They have their **cameras** with them and they too, want a photograph of the monster. The visitors sit on the hills near the Loch or walk along the road beside it. They wait and watch, watch and wait. Who is going to photograph the strange creature in Loch Ness?

水怪照片

CD＊11

　　這時候眾人紛紛說：「我們要尼斯湖水怪的照片。牠到底是魚、奇怪的生物或龍？到底是什麼？」

　　只有照片能夠回答這個問題。「我們要尼西的照片。」

　　報社的編輯同意眾人的話。「照片十分重要。」他們告訴記者們。

　　「去拍一張水怪的照片。」

　　不僅報社記者想要尼西的照片，從英格蘭、威爾斯和愛爾蘭來的遊客湧進尼斯湖，隨身帶著相機，他們也想拍一張水怪的照片。遊客坐在湖邊的山丘上，或沿著湖邊道路走動。他們等待和觀察——觀察和等待。有誰能拍到尼斯湖裡的奇怪生物？

photograph (*n.*)
照片、相片

visitor (*n.*)
訪客、遊客

camera (*n.*)
照相機

A strange creature

CD＊12

Nessie waits too, in the deep water of the Loch. Does she watch the visitors with their cameras? Does she ask, "Who are these strange people? What have they got in their hands?"

One day a man goes to a newspaper editor, "I have it," he says. "I have a photograph of the Loch Ness Monster."

It **shows** Nessie in the year 1934 in the water of Loch Ness. This is the strange creature of the Loch.

水怪游過，在湖面上留下一連串漣漪。（A. Hepburn 攝）▶▶▶

奇怪的生物

CD * 12

尼西也在湖水深處等待。「她」也在觀察帶著相機的遊客嗎？「她」是否在問：「這些奇怪的人是誰？他們手上拿著什麼玩意兒？」

某日，一個男子找上報社編輯。「我有了，」他說：「我有拍到一張尼斯湖水怪的照片。」

那是一九三四年，照片顯示尼西在尼斯湖水中的模樣，這就是湖中的奇怪生物。

show (*v.*)
顯示

The real Nessie?

CD * 13

But is it the real Nessie?

Different photographs are soon in the newspapers.

"This is the Loch Ness Monster," one newspaper says, and shows a photograph.

"No, this is Nessie," a different newspaper tells people, and it shows a different photograph.

"Are they photographs of different creatures? Are they photographs of the monster?" People ask that question and they get different answers from their friends.

"Yes, the photographs show a strange animal." is one answer.

A different answer is, "No, that's a tree in the water."

Or," That's a boat."

Or, "That's a fish. A big fish, but not a monster."

The newspapers say, "It's a mystery—the mystery of Loch Ness.

真的尼西？

CD＊13

但是，這是真的尼西嗎？

不久，各家報紙上刊出不同的照片。

「這是尼斯湖水怪。」一家報紙作出報導並登出照片。

「不對，這才是尼西。」另一家報紙告訴人們，同時登出不同的照片。

「這些是不同生物的照片？這些是水怪的照片？」有人如此問，但他們從朋友那兒得到不同的回答。

「是的，照片裡看得出是一隻奇怪的動物。」其中一個回答。

另一回答是：「不對，那是一棵樹在水中。」

或，「那是一艘船。」

或，「那是一條魚，一條大魚，而不是水怪。」

報上說：這是個謎──尼斯湖之謎。

The mystery remains.

CD＊14

Years come and go, and the mystery of Loch Ness **remains** a mystery. From 1939 to 1945, people do not speak of the strange creature in the Loch. These are **war** years and the newspapers have important stories of the war.

Is it the end of the Loch Ness Monster story? No, it isn't. Nessie remains in the deep water of Loch Ness. **The war ends** and one day a man and a woman are **walking by** the Loch. The man has his camera with him.

"What's that over there in the water?" the woman asks.

"I don't know," the man says, "but I am going to **take a photograph** of it."

He takes a photograph and shows it to the editor of a newspaper.

依然是謎

CD * 14

　　一年又一年過去，尼斯湖之謎仍然是個謎。從一九三九年至一九四五年間，人們不再提湖裡的那隻奇怪生物。這是戰爭期間，報紙要刊登重要的戰爭報導。

　　尼斯湖水怪的報導到此為止嗎？不，還沒完呢。尼西依然留在尼斯湖的水底深處。直到戰爭結束，有一天，一男一女走路經過湖邊，男子身上帶了相機。

　　「那邊水裡面是什麼東西？」女子問。

　　「我不知道，」男子說：「不過，我要拍一張照片。」

　　他拍下照片，拿給報社編輯看。

remain (*v.*)
依然存在

war (*n.*)
戰爭

the war ends
戰爭結束

walk by
走路經過

take a
photograph
照相、拍照片

It is a monster 那就是水怪

CD＊15

Soon people are speaking again of the Loch Ness Monster.

Visitors come to the Loch again. They have new cameras and take good, clear photographs.

In one picture, you can see the **castle beside** the Loch. The castle is big and the creature in the water is big, too. It is a monster!

不久，人們又開始談起尼斯湖水怪。

遊客再度湧入尼斯湖，帶著新相機，拍下明顯清晰的照片。

其中一張照片，你可以看到湖邊的古堡。古堡巍然，而水中的生物也大得可觀。的確是水怪！

castle (*n.*)
古堡、城堡

beside (*prep.*)
在旁邊。

尼斯湖畔的古堡。（成寒 攝）

A movie of the Loch Ness Monster

CD * 16

Now people come to Loch Ness with **movie cameras** and **tape recorders**. They are going to make a movie. Nessie is going to be in the movies and on television. The monster is going to be a **movie star**! The men and women with the movie cameras wait beside the Loch or **go up and down** the Loch in boats. Their movie cameras are ready. Their tape recorders are ready. But Nessie isn't ready.

The monster remains in deep water. People want movies, but does Nessie want them? We like television, but does the Loch Ness Monster like it?

尼斯湖水怪電影

CD ＊ 16

　　這時候人們來到尼斯湖，帶著攝影機和錄音機。他們打算拍電影，尼西將上電影和電視。水怪將要成為電影明星！眾人帶著攝影機在湖邊等待，或搭船在湖面來回。他們的攝影機已經準備好。他們的錄音機也準備好，可是尼西卻還沒。

　　水怪依然留在水底深處。人們想要拍電影，可是尼西願意嗎？我們喜歡電視，可是尼斯湖水怪喜歡嗎？

movie camera
攝影機

tape recorder
錄音機

movie star
電影明星

go up and down
上上下下

Movie star

CD * 17

The men and women with movie cameras say, "We cannot make our film. We don't have our movie star."

They wait beside the Loch and wait and wait.

One man with the movie camera and the tape recorder is Tim Dinsdale. In 1960 he is watching beside Loch Ness.

"What's that over there?" he says one day. "Yes, it's the monster. It's Nessie." Soon, people are watching Tim Dinsdale's movie on television. They can see a creature in the water, but what is it? It's not clear.

Nessie is in a movie and on television, but the mystery remains.

電影明星

CD＊17

　　帶攝影機的這些人說：「我們沒辦法拍電影，因為少了電影明星。」

　　他們在湖邊等了又等。

　　其中一個帶攝影機和錄音機的男子是提姆‧丁斯岱爾（1924-1987）。一九六○年，他守在尼斯湖畔觀察。

　　「那邊是什麼東西？」某日他說：「是的，那就是水怪，那是尼西。」不久，人們在電視上看到提姆‧丁斯岱爾拍的影片。他們可以看到水中有隻生物，可是那到底是什麼？看不太清楚。

　　尼西拍成電影，也上了電視，但依然是個謎。

Is this the Loch Ness Monster?

CD＊18

"What is Nessie?" people ask.

Is the Loch Ness Monster a kind of **plesiosaur**? Plesiosaurs don't live in our lakes today. They are creatures from the past. But do they live in one or two lakes deep down in the water? Does a kind of plesiosaur live in Loch Ness? Is Nessie a creature from the past? That question is important.

Newspaper editors like the mystery of the Loch Ness Monster story. But scientists don't like mysteries. They want **facts**.

這是尼斯湖水怪？

CD＊18

「尼西到底是什麼？」人們問。

尼斯湖水怪是一種蛇頸龍嗎？蛇頸龍並不活在今天的湖裡，牠們是久遠以前的生物。然而，牠們有可能活在其中一座或兩座湖的水底深處嗎？一種類似蛇頸龍的生物住在尼斯湖裡？尼西是久遠以前的生物嗎？這是重要的問題。

報社編輯喜歡尼斯湖水怪之謎的報導，可是科學家們不喜歡謎，他們要求真相。

plesiosaur (*n.*)
蛇頸龍

fact (*n.*)
真相、事實

Listen to Nessie

CD * 19

The water of Loch Ness is not clear. Scientists cannot see in the deep water, but they can listen. They put **special** tape recorders into the water and listen. The special tape recorders give facts to the scientists.

They listen and say, "Yes, Loch Ness has a big animal or fish in it."

"What is it? We don't know. But a strange creature is there. That is a fact."

Scientists still listen with their special tape recorders in the water of Loch Ness. People still watch the Loch. They watch and wait.

Is the monster there too, deep in the water, watching and waiting?

監聽尼西

CD * 19

尼斯湖的水並不清澈。科學家無法看清湖的深處，但他們可以監聽偵測。他們把特製錄音機放進水裡監聽，這種特製錄音機提供科學家事實的真相。

他們監聽之後說：「是的，尼斯湖有大型動物或魚在裡頭。」

「到底是什麼？我們不清楚。但是，的確有奇怪的生物在那裡。這就是真相。」

科學家一直以特殊錄音機在監聽尼斯湖底下的動靜。人們也還在觀察尼斯湖，他們觀察和等待。

水怪也是一樣嗎？在水底深處，觀察和等待？

special (*adj.*)
特別的、特殊的；專門的

Nessie in Business

CD * 20

In Inverness you can buy Nessie. You can buy a picture of Nessie or a Loch Ness Monster book. You can buy a Loch Ness Monster game. You can wear Nessie. You can have a Nessie in your house. The Loch Ness Monster is not only a mystery, it's good **business**.

Visitors to Scotland always go to Loch Ness. They always see the Loch Ness Monster in the shops of Inverness. The people of Inverness like Nessie. The monster is big business.

對因佛尼斯的居民來說，
水怪是賺錢的生意。
（Holly Wallace 攝）

尼西生意

　　在因佛尼斯鎮上，你可以買到尼西。你可以買到尼西的圖片或以尼斯湖水怪為題材的書，你可以買到尼斯湖水怪的遊戲，你可以穿上尼西。你可以把尼西帶回家。尼斯湖水怪不只是個謎，牠是賺錢的生意。

　　造訪蘇格蘭的遊客一定會到尼斯湖，他們總會在因佛尼斯的店舖裡看到尼斯湖水怪。因佛尼斯鎮民都喜歡尼西，因為水怪是大生意。

business (*n.*)
生意

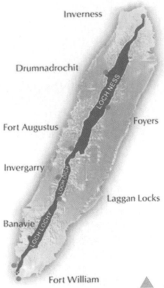

從地圖上可看出，因佛尼斯位於尼斯湖的北邊。

Nessie is?

CD＊21

And that is the Loch Ness Monster—different things to different people. Nessie is a monster or a dragon? It's a big fish or a plesiosaur—a creature from the past? Or it isn't a creature? The photographs are only pictures of trees in the water.

Or boats?

Or birds?

No, the scientists tell us, "Nessie is real. A strange creature lives in the deep water of Loch Ness."

But who is Nessie? What is Nessie? Those questions remain.

That is the mystery of Loch Ness.

夜暮低垂，尼斯湖平靜的湖面下到底有什麼在活動？（成寒 攝）▶▶▶

尼西到底是什麼？

CD ＊ 21

　　而，這就是尼斯湖水怪——不同的人有不同的看法。尼西是水怪或是龍？是魚或蛇頸龍——一種久遠以前的生物？或根本不是生物？照片中只是水中樹的影像？

　　或是船？

　　或是鳥？

　　不對，科學家告訴我們：「尼西是真的，一隻奇怪的生物住在尼斯湖的深水底處。」

　　可是，尼西是誰？尼西是什麼？這些問題依然存在。

　　這是尼斯湖之謎。

中英有聲解說

CD＊22

Key words:

mystery 謎、神祕

loch 湖

monster 怪物

Is the Loch Ness monster real? 尼斯湖水怪是真的嗎？

word 字

Scottish 蘇格蘭的

English 英格蘭的

CD＊23

A loch is a kind of lake in Scotland, a lake between two hills. "loch" 是蘇格蘭地區，夾在兩座山丘之間的湖。

Loch Ness is not the only loch in Scotland, but it is a famous loch. 尼斯湖不是蘇格蘭唯一的湖，卻是一座有名的湖。

Loch Ness is in northern Scotland and Scotland is part of the United Kingdom. 尼斯湖位於蘇格蘭北邊，而蘇格蘭是「英國」的一部分。

speak of 提及、談到

People often speak of Great Britain. 人們經常提及大不列顛。

England 英格蘭

CD＊24

Wales 威爾斯

Scotland 蘇格蘭

Northern Ireland 北愛爾蘭

Scotsman 蘇格蘭人（單數）

kilt 蘇格蘭花格短裙

bagpipe 蘇格蘭風笛

highland 高地

But Scottish people are always Scottish, not English. 但是蘇格蘭人永遠是蘇格蘭人，不是英格蘭人。

CD＊25

Loch Ness is an old lake. 尼斯湖是一座古老的湖。

scientist 科學家

kilometer 公里

38.6 kilometers 38.6 公里

meter 公尺

feet 英尺、呎（foot 的複數）

975 feet deep 975 英尺深、975 呎深

The water in the Loch isn't clear. 尼斯湖的水並不清澈。

CD＊26

What is in the deep water of the Loch? 尼斯湖的深水底下是什麼？

The Inverness Courier is the name of a newspaper. 因佛尼斯快報是一家報紙的名稱。

headline 頭條新聞

spectacle 奇觀

creature 生物

dragon 龍

CD＊27

editor 編輯

important 重要的

question 問題

different 不同的

neck 脖子

hump 隆起的背、駝峰

seal 海豹

whale 鯨魚

draw 畫

CD＊28

photography 攝影

photograph 相片

agree with 同意

visitor 訪客

camera 照相機

Years come and go. 一年又一年過去。

CD＊29

war 戰爭

The war ends. 戰爭結束。

walking by 走路經過

take a photograph 照相

castle 古堡、城堡

CD＊30

tape recorders 錄音機（複數）

They are going to make a movie. 他們要拍電影。

movie star 電影明星

go up and down 上上下下

plesiosaur 蛇頸龍

They want facts. 他們要求真相。

It's good business. 它是賺錢的生意。

尼斯湖水怪之謎

延伸閱讀

Further Reading

尼西—眞實或虛構？
Nessie — Fact or Fiction?

The world famous Loch Ness Monster, known affectionately as "Nessie" by most people and by the scientific believers as **Nessiteras rhombopteryx** goes back a long, long way, the first recorded **sighting** being by **no less a person than a holy saint**. The saint was St. Columba and the year 565 **A.D.**.

Although the largely undocumented St. Ninian is credited with bringing Christianity to the area 100 years before Columba, Saint Columba himself is credited with bringing Christianity to the Scottish nation. When Columba was traveling in the Loch Ness area converting **the heathen Picts**, he came upon some Picts burying a man who had been **ravaged** by a "monster of the water". St. Columba miraculously **restored the man to life** by laying his **staff** across the man's chest.

The next time that any reference to the monster surfaced, was in a letter to "*The Scotsman*" newspaper in 1933 from Mr. D. Murray Rose. He tells of a story in an old book that spoke of the slaying of dragons and the paper goes on to say that Fraser killed the last known dragon in Scotland, but no one has yet managed to slay the monster of Loch Ness lately seen.

The story referred to is dated around 1520, but the letter to the newspaper in 1933 started **a spate of** references to "**leviathans** in the loch" and a host of sightings of the fabled monster. This was encouraged by the new road－now the A82－that was being blasted along the north side of Loch Ness and afforded an unimpaired

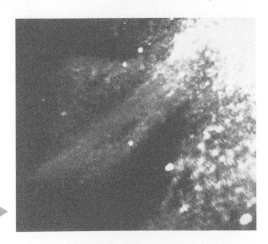

半身沒在水面下的
巨大動物的背部。

view of the whole of the loch. In 1933, **a couple** were driving along the new road. According to their account they saw in the centre of the loch "an enormous animal rolling and plunging."

The report in *the Inverness Courier* **started the ball rolling**. Next, it was published in the Scottish national newspapers and "experts" in photography and other such skills came to the loch to find the monster. Later, *the Daily Mail* announced that it was to **engage** a famous "**big game**" hunter to track down Nessie. Even the Prime Minister, Ramsay MacDonald, planned a trip to the loch in the hope of catching a glimpse of the monster.

On 21st of December, 1933, *the Daily Mail* carried the headline: "Monster of Loch Ness is not a Legend but a Fact." The hunter, M. A. Wetherall, fellow of the Royal Geographical Society and the London Zoological Society said: "It is a four fingered beast and it has feet or

pads of eight inches across. I judge it to be a powerful soft footed animal about 20 feet in length...." Other newspapers **smelled a rat**, launched into the **fray** not only to **pooh-pooh the story**, but to ridicule it also. In fact, it turned out to be a **hoax**, when the so-called hunter had helped his "story" by creating fake footprints.

Since then to the present day there have been many accounts of sightings. Such "evidence" as film footage of Nessie's humps traveling across the Loch and the famous **"Surgeon's" photograph** taken by R. K. Wilson in 1934 have all since turned out to be fakes.

一千五百年前，蘇格蘭高地留存至今的不知名動物浮雕。

Sonar surveys of the Loch using the latest equipment have failed to find any conclusive evidence of Nessie's existence, but neither have they proved that she doesn't exist. Some accounts may well have been sighted **through the bottom of a whisky glass**, but there are still a remarkable number of eye witness accounts that ring true.

Also, the "monster in the loch" **phenomena** seem to be spreading. A lake as far away as Japan now claims it has its own monster and the latest to join the "monster in a lake" set is Lake Van, a **salt water lake** in South Eastern Turkey.

Loch Ness has many **moods** from the sultry to the serene. Strange currents move across and below the

surface and even **sturgeons** and dolphins have been known to swim across the Loch, so who knows what people have seen or not seen. You have to

make up your own mind whether Nessie swims freely through those dark waters or not. There are very few of us however, who do not occasionally stare out across the loch─just in case something strange might break the surface.

內文提示：

Nessiteras rhombopteryx 自然學家彼得‧史考特爵士（Sir Peter Scott）特別為尼斯湖水怪取的學名

sighting （*n.*）目睹、目擊

no less a person than a saint 不是一個普通人而己，更是個聖人

A.D. 從耶穌降生之年算起；西元...年（拉丁文 Anno Doimini 的縮寫）

the heathen Picts 不信奉上帝的野蠻民族─匹克特族

ravage （*v.*）蹂躪

restore the man to life 讓他起死回生

staff （*n.*）拐杖

a spate of 大量的

leviathan （*n.*）巨大的海獸

a couple 一對夫婦

start the ball rolling 觸發整件事情、起了開頭

engage （*v.*）雇用

big game 大型獵物

smell a rat 感到事情不妙、覺得可疑

fray （*n.*）爭執、爭吵、舌戰

pooh-pooh the story 原指撲撲熊「小熊維尼」，在本文中意指：認為這種報導是不重要的、沒什麼意義

hoax （*n.*）惡作劇、騙局

Surgeon's photograph 「外科醫生照片」──倫敦外科醫生威爾森拍的水怪照片，後經電腦分析，證明是假的。請參考本書有聲故事內文的圖片。

through the bottom of a whisky glass 因酒醉而頭昏眼花，看不清楚

phenomena（phenomenon 的複數）現象

salt water lake 鹹水湖

mood （*n.*）心情、情緒、氣氛

make up your own mind 自己拿定主意、自己決定

sturgeon （*n.*）鱘魚

關於尼斯湖之謎
The Riddle of Loch Ness

Whatever it is that stirs in Loch Ness, it is no new-comer. An inscription on a 14th century map of the Loch tells vaguely, but **chillingly**, of "**waves without wind, fish without fins, islands that float**".

"Monster" sightings are not limited to Loch Ness; Lochs Awe, Rannoch, Lomond and Morar have all been said to contain specimens. The Loch Ness Monster owes its greater fame to the open-ing of a main road along the north shore of the loch in 1933. Since then, distant views of "four shining black humps", "brownish-

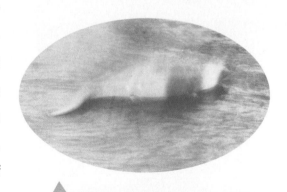

一隻龐然巨物悄然從湖中升起，濺起一連串的水花和泡沫。（Hugh Gray 攝）

grey humps", "a wave" that shoots across the Loch at 20 **mph**, have kept visitors flocking to the Loch.

People who have seen the phenomenon, more closely say that it is "**slug-like**" or "eel-like", with a head resembling a seal's or a gigantic snail's, while the long neck is embellished with a **horse's mane**. Its length has been estimated at anything between 25 ft and 70 ft, and its skin texture is "**warty**" and "**slimy**".

一直以來，蘇格蘭流傳著水怪的傳說。

So far, the creature has presented itself only in glimpses. To believers it has been an unknown fish, a giant slug and a Plesiosaurus. Un-believers are equally imaginative. They suggest that the "monster" is really a tree trunk, or a whale, or a group of **otters** playing "follow the leader".

It is not surprising that such waters, cupped in **savage** hills, should produce legends. Loch Ness is part of the Great Glen, a **geological fault** that **slashes** across Scotland like a **sword-cut.**

尼斯湖四周是荒涼的山丘，成了各種傳說的溫床。

Stories of a "beast" in Loch Ness date back at least to the 6th century. It is recorded in Adamnan's biography of St. Columba that in A.D. 565 the saint prevented a River Ness water monster from eating a Pict. According to another legend, the beast towed St. Columba's boat across the water, and was granted **perpetual freedom** of the loch.

Over the past 70 years, sightings have been claimed by more than 1000 people. Though many of the sightings were from a distance, witnesses have been convinced they were looking at a large animal, most of whose body was hidden beneath the water.

If it exists, it is most unlikely that the Loch Ness monster is a single animal. A prehistoric creature, living alone in Loch Ness, cut off from others of its kind, would have to be millions of years old. For the species to survive there must be quite a large **colony**; **discrepancies** in reported sizes could be accounted for by the presence of adults and young.

The mystery of the Loch Ness Monster continues; and it is perhaps more exciting than any final scientific solution.

内文提示：

chillingly（*adv.*）令人毛骨悚然地

waves without wind, fish without fins, islands that float 無風起浪，有魚無鰭，有島會漂

mph 時速…哩（miles per hour）

slug-like（*adj.*）像蛞蝓的

horse's mane 馬鬃

warty（*adj.*）多疣的

slimy（*adj.*）覆有黏液的

otter（*n.*）海獺

savage（*adj.*）荒涼的、蠻荒的

geological fault 地質的斷層

slash（*v.*）砍、劈

sword-cut 劍傷

perpetual freedom 自由使用權

colony（*n.*）聚落、群體

discrepancy（*n.*）差異、不一致

蘇格蘭的點點滴滴

蛇 頸 龍

　　恐龍時代一種吃魚、產卵的爬蟲類，七千萬年前已經絕種。這種巨獸適於在大海中生存，體長達三十呎。軀體像大木桶，四肢像划槳，頸部細長，頭很小，大嘴巴，牙齒尖銳。

Plesiosaurs were magnificent **ocean-dwelling reptiles** that "flew" gracefully through the water with massive **paddles**. They were **around** almost as long as the dinosaurs from the **Triassic** period 220 million years ago until the end of the **Cretaceous** 65 million years ago. Their **remains** have been found on every **continent**.

Plesiosaurs were one of the first kinds of **extinct** animal known to science, and were described as early as 1821. The smallest were about 2m long as adults. The largest were up to 20m long, **comparable in size** or even bigger than **sperm whales**. They were possibly the biggest **predators** of all time, though **remains of** **these giants** are rare and **fragmentary**, and much research **remains to be done**.

▲

蛇頸龍化石。

内文提示：

ocean-dwelling reptile 居住在海中的爬蟲類

paddle（*n.*）鰭狀前肢

around（*adv.*）在這個地區；活躍著（本文中指「存在於地球上」）

Triassic（*adj.*）三疊紀的（此字亦可作名詞用）

Cretaceous（*n.*）白堊紀（此字亦可作形容詞用）

remains（*n.pl.*）遺骨、遺骸（通常用複數形）

continent（*n.*）大陸（如非洲、南極洲、亞洲、澳洲、歐洲、北美洲、以及南美洲）

extinct（*adj.*）滅絕的、絕跡的

comparable in size 尺寸相當的

sperm whale（*n.*）抹香鯨

predator（*n.*）掠奪者、肉食動物

remains of these giants 這些龐然大物的遺骸

fragmentary（*adj.*）不完整的、零碎的

remain to be done 依然有待完成

忠狗巴比

　　很久以前，小學課本裡有一篇文章談到愛丁堡的忠狗巴比，這是一隻斯開島出產的玩賞犬。十九世紀時最初用途是捕鼠、獵兔，現今則作為主人的夥伴。

　　這篇真實的故事敘述在主人死後，巴比忠心耿耿守候在墳旁長達十四年，直到生命終了，當地人把牠葬在主人隔鄰的墓園裡。

　　許多年後，我來到愛丁堡，當地果然真的有那隻狗，我還無意中在街角撞見了牠的紀念銅像。當地也有一間酒吧，取名巴比。一九六一年，這個故事改編成電影"Greyfriars Bobby"。

　　The small **bronze statue** of Greyfriars Bobby can be found in Candlemakers **Row**, immediately **adjacent** to **Greyfriars Kirkyard**. Greyfriars Bobby was a **Skye terrier** who, upon the death of his master John Gray in 1858, stood guard over his master's grave for over 14

years until his own death in 1872. The **loyalty** of the little dog attracted such deep public **sentiment** that a bronze statue was erected in his memory.

內文提示：

bronze statue 銅像

row 街道、地區（尤指有成排的同類房屋或店舖的街道）

adjacent（*adj.*）鄰近的

Greyfriars（*n.*）灰衣僧：即聖芳濟修會修道士（Franciscans），因他們的道袍為灰色而有此俗稱。

kirkyard（*n.*）教堂墓園（= churchyard）

Skye（*n.*）地名，斯開島（Isle of Skye）

terrier（*n.*）㹴犬

loyalty（*n.*）忠誠、忠心

sentiment（*n.*）感情、情緒

> 34 Candlemaker Row（製蠟燭人街34號）的巴比酒吧。（成寒 攝）

> 忠狗巴比的銅像屹立在愛丁堡的街角。（成寒 攝）

蘇格蘭的點點滴滴
風笛的由來

　　風笛原是牧羊人或農夫的玩意兒，現在卻成為蘇格蘭的象徵樂器。

　　The bagpipes were **instruments** of the **"common" people**－ they were used, probably somewhat roughly without concern, outdoors. People did not collect them, or hang them on a wall －and even if someone **tucked away** grandpa's pipes, poor storage conditions would have been the end of them **before long**.

　　Because in most times and cultures bagpipes were peasant instruments and associated with persons of low **social status** such as **shepherds** and farmers and even **Gypsies**－not much seems to ever have been written about them.

　　There are numerous wind instruments visible in very old Mediterranean and Asian art. But bagpipes are just about invisible, until the **late middle ages** when suddenly, as if **out of nowhere**, they appear in all sorts of artwork. Perhaps during the hundreds of years of the "**Dark Ages**" these peasant instruments continued to develop locally and even spread to some extent, without being recorded. This is of course **speculative**, but it would **account for** the apparently sudden appearance of many quite different forms of bagpipes as Europe emerged from that **dismal** period.

這些風笛的插圖出現於1221-1284 A.D.

內文提示：

instrument（*n.*）樂器

common people　普通人

tuck away　收藏

before long　不久

social status　社會地位、社會身分

shepherd（*n.*）牧羊人

Gypsy（*n.*）吉普賽人

late middle ages　中世紀末期

out of nowhere　不知從哪兒冒出來的

Dark Ages（歐洲史上的）黑暗時代：文化停滯的中世紀
（Middle Ages）時代，尤指西元476-1000年前後。

speculative（*adj.*）推測性的

account for　解釋、說明

dismal（*adj.*）陰鬱的、黯淡的

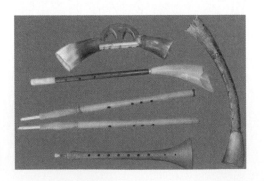

各式各樣的風笛。

蘇格蘭的點點滴滴
花格短裙的花樣

　　從蘇格蘭短裙上條紋及格子圖案及顏色的不同，可看出屬於不同的家族。

　　The **tartan** kilt has long been the most recognizable cultural tradition of the Highland **Scots**. Every tartan today features a **multicolored** arrangement of **stripes** and **checks**. Therefore, it surprises most people that many of the most recognizable features and traditions associated with the wearing of the kilt have, in fact, been developed in the nineteenth century, not by **Scottish Highlanders**, but by the **Nobles** of England and Scotland.

　　There is much evidence that many of the more recognizable tartans seen today are in fact creations of Scottish and English **tailors** during the **reign** of Queen Victoria. Despite this, it has generally been accepted

that the basic concepts of the tartan and the wearing of the kilt do indeed have their origin in the history of the early Scottish and Irish **clans**, or families.

It is generally recognized that the first tartans were the result of individual **weavers** own designs, then were slowly adopted to identify individual **districts**, then finally clans and families. These **patterns** are used to identify the clan, family, or **regiment** with which the wearer is associated. The kilt has now become the standard dress for all "Highlanders".

内文提示：

tartan（*n.*）花格圖案（各種顏色的格子條紋圖案，原為蘇格蘭家族的紋章圖案）

Scot（*n.*）蘇格蘭人（Scotsman）

multicolored（*adj.*）多色的

stripe（*n.*）條紋圖案

check（*n.*）格子圖案

Scottish Highlander 蘇格蘭高地人

noble（*n.*）貴族

tailor（*n.*）裁縫

reign（*n.*）在位時期、統治時期

clan（*n.*）（以前蘇格蘭高地人的）氏族

weaver（*n.*）織工

district（*n.*）地區

pattern（*n.*）花樣

regiment（*n.*）軍團

穿著格子裙的蘇格蘭男子。（成寒攝）

農夫詩人彭斯

　　即使你未曾聽過蘇格蘭詩人彭斯（Robert Burns, 1759-1796）的名字，但你一定聽過根據他的詩改編的一首歌＜驪歌＞（Auld Lang Syne）。

Should auld acquaintance be forgot,
故人是否就應該被遺忘，
And never brought to mind?
永遠不會再想起？
Should auld acquaintance be forgot,
故人是否就應該被遺忘，
And days of auld lang syne?
遺忘昔日美好的時光？

（註：蘇格蘭語 auld lang syne = old long ago）

　　彭斯出身佃農之家，因此有人稱他為「農夫詩人」（The Ploughman Poet）。他能以十八世紀的英文和傳統的蘇格蘭方言創作，題材多面向，有情歌＜一朵紅紅的玫瑰＞（*A Red, Red Rose*）、對受驚嚇小鼠的同情（*To a Mouse*）、鼓舞蘇格蘭民心＜蘇格蘭人＞（*Scots Wha' Hae*）甚至一般人的頌辭。他那首＜寫給小鼠＞的名句：

人也罷，鼠也罷，最如意的安排

也不免常出意外！

The best-laid schemes o' mice an' men

Gang aft agley,

彭斯畫像。

　　日後，一九六二年諾貝爾文學獎得主史坦貝克（John Steinbeck, 1902-1968）借來當書名《人鼠之間》（*Of Mice and Men*）。

　　一七九六年，彭斯因風濕性心臟病而過世，享年三十七歲。

每年元月二十五日彭斯誕辰，世界各地的蘇格蘭人為了紀念他特別舉辦「彭斯之夜」（Burns Night）。

＊蘇格蘭另有兩名國際知名作家，包括《金銀島》（*Treasure Island*）作者史蒂文生（Robert Louis Stevenson, 1850-1894），以及曾拍成電影《劫後英雄傳》（*Ivanhoe*）的作者司各特（Walter Scott, 1771-1832）。

The best known and most often sung of all songs, reminds us that Burns is as much the poet of friendship as of love. This was one of many traditional Scottish songs which Burns collected and **rewrote**.

On 17th December 1788, Burns said in a letter to Mrs. Dunlop: "Your meeting which you so well describe with your old **schoolfellow** and friend was truly interesting. There is an old song and **tune** which has often **thrilled** through my soul. You know I am an **enthusiast** in old Scotch songs. I shall give you the **verses** on the other sheet..."

The song "on the other sheet" was Burns's first **version** of "Auld Lang Syne".

Later Robert Burns sent a copy of the original song

to the **British Museum** with this **comment**: "The following song, an old song, of the olden times, and which has never been **in print**, nor even in **manuscript** until I took it down from an old man's singing, is enough to recommend any **air**."

Of course Auld Lang Syne is more than a New Year's song. It is one of the great expressions of the tragic **ambiguity** of man's relation to time, which mixes memory with desire, carrying away old friendships and bringing new, turning childhood escapades into old men's **recollections**, changing the very condition of **consciousness**, and at the same time the creator and the destroyer of human experience.

彭斯出生於 Alloway，
小小的茅草農舍，如
今已成立紀念館。
（成寒 攝）

內文提示：

rewrite（*v.*）改寫（過去式及過去分詞rewrote,rewritten）

schoolfellow（*n.*）同學（＝schoolmate）

tune（*n.*）調子、曲調、歌曲

thrill（*v.*）震顫、激動

enthusiast（*n.*）...狂、...迷

verse（*n.*）詩句

version（*n.*）版本

British Museum 大英博物館

comment（*n.*）評註、解說

in print 出版的（out of print 絕版的）

manuscript（*n.*）手稿

air（*n.*）曲調、旋律

ambiguity（*n.*）曖昧、不明確

recollection（*n.*）回憶

consciousness（*n.*）知覺、意識

發明電話的人

貝爾終生研究與聲音有關的東西，但他也研究聽不見聲音的問題。他教耳朵聽不見的人說話，學讀唇語，其中一位女學生後來成為他的妻子。當他們的孩子年幼時，十分有教養，從不背對著父母親的臉說話。有許多年，孩子居然不知道母親是個聾子。

A **pioneer** in the field of **telecommunications**, Alexander Graham Bell was born in 1847 in Edinburgh, Scotland. He moved to **Ontario**, and then to the United States, settling in Boston, before beginning his career as an **inventor**.

Throughout his life, Bell had been interested in the education of **deaf** people. This interest **led** him to invent the **microphone** and, in 1876, his "electrical speech machine," which we now call a telephone.

Since his death in 1922, the telecommunication industry has **undergone** an amazing revolution. Today, non-hearing people are able to use a special **display telephone** to communicate. **Fiber optics** is improving the quality and speed of data **transmission**. Bell's "electrical speech machine" **paved the way** for the **Information Superhighway**.

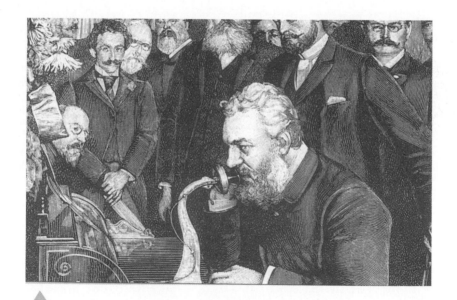

當著大眾面前，貝爾親自展示電話的功用。

內文提示：

pioneer（*n.*）先驅、開路先鋒

telecommunication（*n.*）電信

Ontario（*n.*）（加拿大的）安大略省

inventor（*n.*）發明家

deaf（*adj.*）耳朵聽不見的、聾的

lead（*v.*）領頭、引導（過去式及過去分詞 led）

microphone（*n.*）麥克風

undergo（*v.*）經歷 （過去式及過去分詞underwent,
undergone）

display telephone 顯示型電話

fiber optics 光纖

transmission（*n.*）傳輸

pave the way 鋪路

Information Superhighway 資訊超級高速公路

蘇格蘭的點點滴滴

發明蒸汽機的人

電力的單位「瓦特」，其實是人名。大部分的電燈泡上都印著他的名字。

James Watt was born in Greenock in 1736. He had little **formal education** due to poor health in his youth, but spending his boyhood **constructing models** in the shop of his father's shipbuilding business, he developed an interest in trying to make things "work like **clockwork**".

In his **late teens** he went to London to learn to be a "mathematical and philosophical instrument maker", and when he returned to Glasgow he got a job making instruments with Glasgow University, who gave him **accommodation** and a **workshop**.

In 1763 John Anderson （1726-1796，格拉斯哥大學教授） asked him to repair an early **steam engine** he had acquired. This early model, known as a Newcomen engine, was very **inefficient**. The **cylinder** had to be heated when steam was admitted, and then gradually cooled again to **condense** the steam. This wasted a lot of time and **fuel**.

Two years later, while wandering **aimlessly** through **Glasgow Green**, Watt hit upon the idea of condensing the steam in a separate **vessel**. This removed the need for heating and cooling, making the engine faster, safer, and more efficient. A stone in Glasgow Green marks the **spot** where the **industrial revolution** really began.

In 1882, 63 years after Watt's death, the British Association gave his name to the **unit** of electrical power - and today James Watt's name is to be found written on almost every **light bulb** in the world.

内文提示：

formal education（學校的）正式教育

construct models 製造模型

clockwork（n.）鐘錶裝置、發條裝置

late teens 十八、九歲的時候

accommodation（*n.*）住宿

workshop（*n.*）工作室

steam engine 蒸汽機

inefficient（*adj.*）效率低的

cylinder（*n.*）汽缸

condense（*v.*）凝結

fuel（*n.*）燃料

aimlessly（*adv.*）

無目的地

Glasgow Green

格拉斯哥公園

vessel（*n.*）導管

spot（*n.*）地點

industrial revolution

工業革命

unit（*n.*）單位

light bulb 燈泡

「我發現了！」當瓦特發現蒸汽的神奇力量時，忍不住驚呼出聲。

蘇格蘭的點點滴滴

喬治王時期風格建築

在愛丁堡的舊城區，遍布十八世紀「喬治王時期風格」
（Georgian style, 1714-1837）建築。

Georgian style **embraces** a whole century under
the reign of three **successive** Georges – I, II, III and IV
and is therefore often divid-
ed into three **distinct** peri-
ods: **Palladian**, early and
late Georgian. The style was
partly a reaction to the
excesses of **Baroque** which
George I **loathed**, so when
much of London had to be
rebuilt after **the Great Fire**
in 1666, it was seen as **a
clean slate**.

喬治王時期風格的門。（成寒 攝）

Taking an interest in fashion and **interiors** was very much **the order of the day**; entertaining was becoming more popular and print books containing designs and architectural models were becoming available to the public for the first time. The three phases are a **continuum** of each other and as the century progressed, the style became lighter and lighter **in terms of** colours and decoration and eventually became **Regency style**.

內文提示：

embrace（*v.*）包含

successive（*adj.*）連續的

distint（*adj.*）截然不同的

Palladian（*adj.*）帕拉底歐風格的：指16世紀義大利建築家帕拉底歐（Andrea Palladio）的風格。

excess（*n.*）過度、過分

Baroque（*n.*）巴洛克風格

the Great Fire 倫敦大火

a clean slate（*n.*）（沒有任何不良記錄或污點的）一張白紙：比喻說法；slate原義是寫字用的石板。

loathe（*v.*）厭惡

interior（*n.*）室内、室内裝潢

the order of the day 風潮、流行

continuum（*n.*）連續、延續

in terms of 從…方面而言

Regency style 攝政時期風格

這扇門也是喬治王時期風格，門上的窗別具特色。（成寒 攝）

蘇格蘭的點點滴滴
格拉斯哥藝術學院 & 麥金塔

　　麥金塔的建築深深影響後代，據說美國建築大師萊特(Frank Lloyd Wright)年輕時，有一次參加建築競圖獲獎，後來被批評抄襲自麥金塔的作品。

The history of the **Glasgow School of Art** is **inextricably** linked to Charles Rennie Mackintosh. A graduate of the School, Mackintosh's 1896 design for a

麥金塔肖像

new School of Art building **heralded** the birth of a new style in 20th century European Architecture and remains at the centre of the campus.

　　Charles Mackintosh was born in Glasgow, Scotland in 1868. In 1884 he began an **apprenticeship** with John Hutchinson and also **enrolled** at the Glasgow School of Art.

While enrolled at the Glasgow School of Art, Mackintosh developed an artistic relationship with Margaret MacDonald

(who later became his wife), Frances Macdonald and Herbert McNair. Known as "The Four", they exhibited posters, **furnishings**, and **a variety of** graphic designs in Glasgow, London, **Vienna** and **Turin**. These exhibitions helped establish Mackintosh's reputation.

格拉斯藝術學院

With a design philosophy solidly rooted in Scottish tradition, Mackintosh **disregarded** the architecture of Greece and Rome as unsuitable for the **climate** or needs of Scotland. He believed that a **revival** of the Scottish **Baronial style**, adapted to modern society would **meet contemporary needs**. His buildings clearly demonstrate this belief.

An outstanding architect, furniture designer, and painter, who **pioneered** the Modern Movement in Scotland, Mackintosh's works exist as the greatest flowering of the British **Arts & Crafts movement** in either Scotland or England. Mackintosh died in London in 1928.

＊由蘋果電腦公司（Apple Computers）設計的「麥金塔」，與本文介紹的麥金塔本來無關。然而，當初蘋果電腦「麥金塔」設計者也叫麥金塔（John Macintosh），他出生於紐約，但父親是來自因佛尼斯，也就是尼斯湖水怪的故鄉。

內文提示：

Glasgow School of Art 格拉斯哥藝術學院

inextricably（*adv.*）兩者分不開地、牢不可分地

herald（*v.*）預示、預告

apprenticeship（*n.*）學徒身分、學徒生涯

enroll（*v.*）註冊入學

furnishings（*n.*）室內的陳設品（包括家具、地毯、椅套等)

a variety of 各種、許多種的

Vienna（*n.*）維也納（奧地利首都）

Turin（*n.*）杜林（義大利西部城市）

disregard（*v.*）無視、不顧

climate（*n.*）氣候

revival（*n.*）復興

Baronial style 蘇格蘭地主莊園風格（baron原義為伯爵）

meet contemporary needs 符合當代的需要

pioneer（*v.*）開拓、開創、打前鋒

Arts & Crafts movement 美術與工藝運動

蘇格蘭的點點滴滴
燕麥粥、哈吉斯、韭菜雞肉湯

　　旅行作家摩頓（H.V. Morton, 1892-1979）曾經說過：「世上最能挑起人食慾的地方就是蘇格蘭。」（Scotland is the best place in the world to take an appetite.）這句話，我完全同意。

　　雖然我早就對英格蘭的某些食物失望透頂，尤其是「炸魚薯條」（fish 'n' chips）搭配「水煮豆」（mushy peas），吃過毫無滋味；麵包店裡買來的「腰子派」（kidney pie），冷掉以後散發出一股腥味。

　　誰知來到蘇格蘭，竟又生起胃口來，也許是因為這些蘇格蘭食物從來沒嘗過的緣故。B & B 所提供的早餐，除了我最愛的「全套英式早餐」（Full English breakfast），包括煎煙燻肉、荷包蛋、蘑菇、香腸、煎番茄、烤土司，還有一道熱呼呼的「燕麥粥」（porridge）。晚餐則在當地一家小餐館點了「哈吉斯」（haggis），俗稱「肚包羊雜」，同時來上一道熱湯「韭菜雞肉湯」（cock-a-leekie）或由羊肉原汁、蔬菜、大麥、扁豆熬成的「蘇格蘭高湯」（Scotch broth），趁熱吃下肚，覺得風味頗佳。

每年彭斯之夜，依例年習俗將熱騰騰的哈吉斯端上桌，晚餐伴隨著詩歌吟詠、奏樂以及彭斯的那首詩＜致哈吉斯＞（Address to the Haggis）揭開序幕。

有個蘇格蘭佬告訴我，哈吉斯的烹調方法如下：

Go out and kill a lamb, cut it up, take out the stomach, liver, and the rest of the stuff inside the lamb.

Mix everything and add some salt and pepper, some eggs and last, onion.

Cook it in a big pot for 3-4 hours over an open fire.

Then serve it hot!

宰頭小羊，取出胃、肝和小羊肚子裡的其他東西，

把所有東西混在一起，加進鹽、胡椒、蛋，最後再加洋蔥，

在爐火上用個大鍋煮上三到四小時，

然後，趁熱端上桌！

蘇格蘭民謠

你聽過蘇格蘭民謠嗎？

尼斯湖水怪出現的地點在蘇格蘭的尼斯湖。蘇格蘭男人穿花格短裙、吹風笛，而且還出了一位名氣響亮的第一代○○七情報員詹姆斯‧龐德──史恩‧康納萊（Sean Connery），他那一口特殊的蘇格蘭腔，講話總是帶著蘇格蘭高地的粗喉音（burr）──發音中顫動小舌的 r 音。在電影中，無論他飾演的是什麼角色，如一九八七年拿下奧斯卡最佳男配角的《鐵面無私》（*The Untouchable*）裡的警察，或《獵殺紅色十月》（*The Hunt For Red October*）中的蘇聯叛變艦長或是在《第一武士》（*First Knight*）飾演的亞瑟王，只要一開口，就是蘇格蘭高地特有的英語腔調。

二○○三年英國電影雜誌《帝國》（*Empire*）評論「史恩‧康納萊是影史上最糟糕的口音」（Sean Connery tops list of worst accents in movie history.）。

這也難怪，人家本來就是蘇格蘭人，怎能拿來和正統

「英國腔」（British accent）相提並論呢！不同地方的人本來就說不同的口音，這樣比較是不太公平的。況且，蘇格蘭人從來不承認自己是英國人，幾度想搞獨立呢。

蘇格蘭男子的滑稽漫畫。

　　聽蘇格蘭民謠，你就會發現，連歌詞都不完全像英文，字裡行間經常出現的bonnie，意思是令人愉快的、漂亮的、美麗的。

　　這首著名的蘇格蘭民謠＜羅莽湖邊＞，聽一聽，感受一下不一樣的民俗音樂。

羅莽湖邊
Loch Lomond

By yon bonnie banks and by yon bonnie braes

Where the sun shines bright on Loch Lomond

Where me and my true love were ever wont to gae

On the bonnie, bonnie banks o' Loch Lomond

O ye'll tak' the high road and I'll tak' the low road

And I'll be in Scotland afore ye

But me and my true love will never meet again

On the bonnie, bonnie banks o' Loch Lomond

'Twas there that we parted in yon shady glen

On the steep, steep side o' Ben Lomond

Where in deep purple hue, the hieland hills we view

And the moon comin' out in the gloamin'

The wee birdies sing and the wild flowers spring

And in sunshine the waters are sleeping

But the broken heart, it kens nae second spring again

Tho' the waefu' may cease frae their greeting

O ye'll tak' the high road and I'll tak' the low road

And I'll be in Scotland afore ye

But me and my true love will never meet again

On the bonnie, bonnie banks o' Loch Lomond

美麗的羅莽湖。（吳家恆 攝）

　　這首歌詞據說是一名士兵在臨死前寫給他的愛人。兩名蘇格蘭士兵在異鄉被英軍俘虜後，其中一人被判死刑，另一卻獲得釋放，好讓他回去傳播反抗英軍的下場。將被處死的士兵在歌中說，他的靈魂走黃泉路（the low road），會比戰友走人間路（the high road，或許也指要回到蘇格蘭的崎嶇的山路），更快回到家鄉。

　　歌詞中有些是蘇格蘭語：

braes = hillsides　山坡
gae = go
Ben Lomond　羅莽山
kens nae = knows not
frae = from

　　羅莽湖的歌詞有許多不同版本。這篇是「尼斯湖水怪之謎」有聲書CD中所收錄的古老版本，不過歌者只唱了四段，不包含第三段。

羅莽湖邊

中文歌詞：

出城郊風光好，望遠陂真美麗，
香塵日照裡羅莽湖上，
憶當初雙情侶，終朝攜手共游嬉，
在那美麗美麗羅莽湖上。

憶別離兩依依，無盡語在山谷，
欲去復踟躕羅莽湖上，
日向西山色紫，新月如眉天就暮，
舊景模糊人影孤羅莽湖邊。

鳥聲溢鳴啾唧，野花放遍地香，
湖水映日光增我哀傷，
萬種愁何時休，最是離愁無限長，
如此湖光空眺望羅莽湖上。

你要越高山，我要履平夷，

到鄉關行路難，你來何遲，

哦！哦！雙情侶，從今恐無相見期，

在那美麗美麗羅莽湖眉。

＊本文引自楊鳳鳴編著《高中音樂》；中文譯詞：海舟。

情侶依偎在羅莽湖邊。（成寒 攝）

測　驗

蘇格蘭有山有水，有歌有舞，還有水怪，
很值得去遊覽！不過，現在我們要做測驗了！

Greetings from
Bonnie Scotland

聽力測驗要點
The Mystery of the Loch Ness Monster

字彙量：900字

　　這部實地報導的英語有聲書，一共有21段，文體全部以「現在式」（present tense）書寫，句型結構簡單。

　　你可以一口氣聽完，也可分段來聽，當然更可以躺著聽。然後作填空測驗，把括弧內遺漏掉的字（有的不只一個字）寫下。解答附在每一組內文之後。由於寫的速度比較慢，必須連續放兩遍才做得完填空。

　　最好是在還沒事先「看過」或「聽過」整篇故事之前，先做聽力測驗，看看自己的實力如何。然後再開始邊看書邊聽。

　　記住，先聽幾遍，用耳朵把一些半生不熟的單字「勾」出來，再對照看原文。

　　一開始不要先看內文，以免寵壞了耳朵，它就不管用了。

具戲劇和音效的臨場感，剛開始你也許不太適應，但只要多聽幾遍，耳朵熟能生巧，漸漸就能融會貫通。

聽力小祕訣：至少先聽六遍以上，再翻開書來看。即使不能完全聽懂，也要讓耳朵熟悉英語的聲音與語調。

「悅聽」與「泛聽」對學英文非常重要。大量的聽，且要聽許多遍，而不是抱著一本教科書死啃。學英文要像吃自助餐，不要老吃同一道菜，最好是各色好菜搭配著吃，這樣才不會吃膩。

建議你把家裡的幾套CD有聲書拿出來，替換著聽，一來避免聽膩，二來英語更容易觸類旁通，聽力越練越好，會話也跟著進步。

倘若你的聽力不佳，聽不懂別人說的話，那要如何回答呢？恐怕是「答非所問」。所以要先會聽，就會說，也會寫。

聽有聲書，你會發現，學英語是多麼有趣的過程。你並不需要認識每一個單字，也不必完全聽懂所有的句子，只要抓住幾個「關鍵字」（key words），就能輕鬆享受聽故事的樂趣。

字彙測驗 Vocabulary Test

請從以下字彙中挑出合適的字眼，分別填入相關英英字義解釋的空格裡：

bagpipes   scientist   mystery   kilt   seal
editor   plesiosaur   headline   creature   monster
loch   hump

1.（   ）Scottish word for a lake

2.（   ）a person or animal that is markedly unusual or deformed and abnormally large

3.（   ）something that is not understood and cannot be explained

4.（   ）a type of musical instrument, played especially in Scotland and Ireland

5.（   ）a knee-length pleated tartan skirt worn by men in the Highlands of northern Scotland

6.（   ）a sentence of text at the top of a newspaper article, explaining the nature of the article below it

7.(　　　) something that bulges out from a form, like on the back of a camel

8.(　　　) extinct marine reptile with a small head on a long neck, a short tail and four paddle-shaped limbs

9.(　　　) a person responsible for the editorial aspects of publication

10.(　　　) a person with advanced knowledge of one of the sciences

11.(　　　) a living thing, such as an animal, a bird or an insect

12.(　　　) marine mammals that come on shore to breed; chiefly of cold regions

解答：
1. loch 2. monster 3. mystery 4. bagpipes 5. kilt
6. headline 7. hump 8. plesiosaur 9. editor
10. scientist 11. creature 12. seal

尼斯湖之謎 *The mystery of Loch Ness*

The Loch Ness Monster.

A（1.　　　　） monster.

A famous（2.　　　　）.

Yes, the Loch Ness Monster is a mystery.

People（3.　　　　）,"What is in Loch Ness?"

"Is it a monster?"

"Is the Loch Ness Monster（4.　　　　）?"

People ask those（5.　　　　）, but they don't know the（6.　　　　）. That is the mystery－the mystery of Loch Ness.

This book tells the（7.　　　　） of that mystery. It tells the real story of the Loch Ness Monster.

＊第一段測驗解答：

1. famous　2. mystery　3. ask　4. real　5. questions

6. answers　7. story

＊ 第二段聽力測驗　　　　　　　CD ＊ 2

怪物的定義？ *What is a monster?*

What is a monster?

It's a big（1.　　　　　）or a big（2.　　　　　）. It's big and it's（3.　　　　　）. A（4.　　　　　）animal or fish can be strange,（5.　　　　　）. But we don't say, "that's a monster."

A monster is（6.　　　　　）big.

＊第二段測驗解答：

1. animal 2. fish 3. strange 4. small 5. too
6. always

湖的定義？ *What is a loch?*

It's a strange（1.　　　　）, "loch". It is a（2.　　　　）word. English people say "（3.　　　　）". Scottish people say "loch". A "loch" is a（4.　　　　）of lake in Scotland, a lake（5.　　　　）two hills.

Loch Ness is not（6.　　　　）loch in Scotland, but it is a famous loch. Loch Ness is not the only loch（7.　　　　）a monster, but the Loch Ness Monster is *the* famous monster.

✱第三段測驗解答：

1. word 2. Scottish 3. lake 4. kind 5. between
6. the only 7. with

✱第四段測驗解答：

1. northern 2. part of 3. Wales 4. Northern Ireland
5. Scotsman 6. kilt 7. bagpipes 8. highland dress ▶▶▶
9. also 10. all 11. friend 12. a happy man

蘇格蘭 *Scotland*

Loch Ness is in （1.　　　　　） Scotland and Scotland is （2.　　　　　） the United Kingdom.

People often speak of Great Britain. Great Britain is only England, （3.　　　　　） and Scotland. The United Kingdom is Great Britain and （4.　　　　　）.

You can see a （5.　　　　　）. He is wearing a （6.　　　　　） and playing the （7.　　　　　）. Men and women wear the kilt. It is part of （8.　　　　　）. The bagpipes are （9.　　　　　） Scottish. Scotsmen in the Highlands do not always wear kilts. They do not （10.　　　　　） play bagpipes. But Scottish people are always Scottish, not English.

Say to a Scotsman, "You're Scottish," and he's your （11.　　　　　）.

Say, "you're English, " and he's not （12.　　　　　）.

尼斯湖 *Loch Ness*

"Loch Ness is an old lake," (1.　　　) tell us.

Old? Yes, 25,000 years is old.　It is also a long lake. It is 38.6 (2.　　　)(24 miles) long, but only 1.6 kilometers (1 mile)　(3.　　　). Eight rivers and 228 streams (4.　　　) it. The rivers and streams, small rivers, come down from the hills and the water runs into the Loch.

Loch Ness is also a deep lake, 296 meters (975 feet)　deep. The water in the Loch isn't (5.　　　). You can see into clear water, but Loch Ness has only one (6.　　　) of clear water.

What is (7.　　　) that? What is in the deep water of the Loch? That is the mystery of Loch Ness.

＊第五段測驗解答：

1. scientists 2. kilometers 3. across 4. run into
5. clear 6. meter 7. under

尼西 *Nessie*

　　The Loch Ness Monster has a（1.　　　　　）. The monster is in Loch Ness, and the name of the monster is Nessie. Nessie is a real Scottish name and it is not only the name of the monster. Nessie（2.　　　　　） the name Agnes. Agnes－Nessie. Scottish people like the name Agnes and it is（3.　　　　　） in Scotland. Nessie is common, too.

　　The name of Loch Ness comes from the River Ness.　It runs from Loch Ness to the（4.　　　　　） of Inverness. Inverness is（5.　　　　　） of the River Ness.

＊第六段測驗解答：

1. name　2. comes from　3. common　4. town

5. mouth

因佛尼斯快報 *The Inverness Courier*

The Inverness Courier is the name of a (1.   ). The people of Inverness (2.   ) it. One day, in the year 1933, they see a (3.   ) in the newspaper:

"Strange (4.   ) on Loch Ness! What is it?"

Under this headline is a strange story. "Man and woman see a big (5.   ) in the Loch." it says. "Does a monster live in Loch Ness?"

"The monster story is not new," the newspaper says. "It's an old story, but is it a (6.   )?"

"Yes," people say, "it's true."

People (7.   ) to the newspaper. They (8.   ) the story. Soon a (9.   ) comes from a Mr. Spicer. Mr. and Mrs. Spicer live in (10.   ) but they often go to Scotland. One day, they are in their car (11.   ) Loch Ness and they see the monster. Mr. Spicer's letter tells the story. He agrees with the newspaper.

（接下頁）

"Yes," Mr. Spicer writes. "The monster is there. A strange creature lives in Loch Ness. It's a (12.   )."

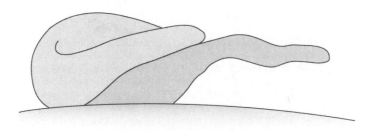

史派瑟（Mr.Spicer）筆下所畫的奇怪生物。

*第七段測驗解答：

1. newspaper 2. read 3. headline 4. spectacle

5. creature 6. true story 7. write 8. agree with

9. letter 10. London 11. near 12. dragon

每日郵報 *The Daily Mail*

The Daily Mail is a newspaper, too. It's a big and (1.   ) London newspaper.

The editor of The Daily Mail sees the letter in the Inverness Courier.

"Strange creature in Loch Ness." he reads. "a dragon lives in the Loch." The editor (2.   ) to a reporter, Percy Cater.

"This is a good story," he says. "An important story. But is it a true story? Go to Scotland. Speak to (3.   ) people."

The Daily Mail is going to tell the story of the Loch Ness Monster.

＊第八段測驗解答：

1. important　2. speaks　3. these

不同的說法 *Different stories*

The Daily Mail reporter is（1.　　　　　）. He goes to Scotland and asks（2.　　　　　）. People tell him （3.　　　　　）things.

A man says, "The monster has a long （4.　　　　　） and a big（5.　　　　　）.

But a woman says, "No, it has a（6.　　　　　） neck and a small head."

"It has two（7.　　　　　）," one man tells the reporter.

"The monster has three humps," a different man says.

"Do you have your story?" The editor of The Daily Mail asks Percy Cater.　　　　　（接下頁）

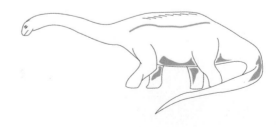

"I have different stories," the reporter says. "The monster has a short neck and a long neck, a big head and a small head. It has two or three humps."

"It's a strange monster. That's true."

水怪有三座駝峰。（Lachlan Stuart 攝）

*第九段測驗解答：

1. happy 2. questions 3. different 4. neck 5. head
6. short 7. humps

水怪圖像 *A picture of the monster*

Percy Cater（1.　　　　　）stories in The Daily Mail. In one story, he says "the creature in the Loch is a （2.　　　　　）. It's not a monster."

But people say, "No, the creature（3.　　　　）a seal."

"The monster is a（4.　　　　），" Percy Cater writes in a（5.　　　　）story.

"Naw, it cannot be a whale," people tell him.

In 1934, a different man, Mr. John McClean sees the creature in the Loch. Mr. McClean can （6.　　　　）and he draws a（7.　　　　）of the monster. It is not a seal or a whale. Soon, the （8.　　　　）of The Daily Mail has Mr.McClean's picture and the headline:

"Monster in the Loch! Mystery of Loch Ness!"

＊第十段測驗解答：

1. writes　2. seal　3. cannot be　4. whale　5. news
6. draw　7. picture　8. front page

水怪照片 *A photograph of the monster*

Nessie, the Loch Ness Monster is famous!

Now people say, "We want a (1.　　　) of the Loch Ness Monster. Is it a (2.　　　), a strange creature, a dragon? What is it?"

Only a photograph can answer that question. "We want a photograph of Nessie."

The editors of newspapers agree with the people. "A photograph is important," they tell the reporters.

"Get a photograph of the monster."

Not only the newspaper reporters want a photograph of Nessie. (3.　　　) come to Loch Ness from England, Wales and Ireland. They have their (4.　　　) with them and they too, want a photograph of the monster. The visitors (5.　　　) the

（接下頁）

hills（6.　　　　）the Loch or walk（7.　　　　）the road beside it. They wait and watch, watch and wait. Who is going to photograph the strange creature in Loch Ness?

＊第十一段測驗解答：

1. photograph 2. fish 3. Visitors 4. cameras
5. sit on 6. near 7. along

奇怪的生物 *A strange creature*

Nessie waits too, in the deep water of the Loch. Does she watch the visitors with their cameras? Does she ask, "Who are these strange people? What have they (1.   ) in their (2.   )?"

One day a man goes to a newspaper (3.   ), "I have it," he says. "I have a photograph of the Loch Ness Monster."

It shows Nessie in the year (4.   ) in the water of Loch Ness. This is the strange creature of the Loch.

✻ 第十段測驗解答：

1. got 2. hands 3. editor 4. 1934

眞的尼西？ *The real Nessie?*

But is it the real Nessie?

Different photographs are (1.　　　　) in the newspapers.

"This is the Loch Ness Monster," one newspaper says, and (2.　　　　) a photograph.

"No, this is Nessie," a different newspaper tells people, and it shows a different photograph.

Are they photographs of different creatures? Are they photographs of the monster? People ask that question and they get different (3.　　　　) from their friends.

"Yes, the photographs show a strange animal." is one answer.

A different answer is, "No, that's a (4.　　) in the water."

（接下頁）

Or, "That's a (5.　　　　　)."

Or, "That's a fish. A big fish, but not a monster."

The newspapers say, "It's a mystery－the mystery of Loch Ness.

水怪游過，在湖面上留下一連串漣漪。（A. Hepburn 攝）

＊第十三段測驗解答：

1. soon　2. shows　3. answers　4. tree　5. boat

聽力測驗

依然是謎 *The mystery remains.*

Years (1.　　　　　), and the mystery of Loch Ness (2.　　　　　) a mystery. From (3.　　　　　), people do not speak of the strange creature in the Loch. These are war years and the newspapers have important stories of the war.

Is it (4.　　　　　) the Loch Ness Monster story? No, it isn't. Nessie remains in the deep water of Loch Ness. The war (5.　　　　　) and one day a man and a woman are (6.　　　　　) the Loch. The man has his camera with him.

"What's that (7.　　　　　) in the water?" the woman asks.

（接下頁）

"I don't know," the man says, "but I am going to
(8. _____) of it."

He takes a photograph and shows it to the editor of
a newspaper.

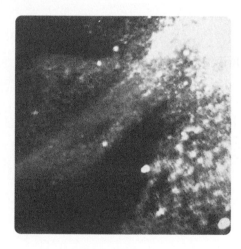

一團黝黑的陰影——
這是尼斯湖水怪嗎？

*第十四段測驗解答：

1. come and go 2. remains 3. 1939 to 1945

4. the end of 5. ends 6. walking by 7. over there

8. take a photograph

✳第十五段聽力測驗　　　　　　CD✳15

那就是水怪 *It is a monster.*

Soon people are speaking (1.　　　) of the Loch Ness Monster.

Visitors come to the Loch again. They have new cameras and take good, (2.　　　) photographs.

In one picture, you can see the (3.　　　) beside the Loch. The castle is big and the creature in the water is big, too. It is a monster!

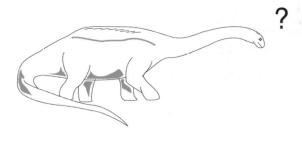

✳第十五段測驗解答：

1. again　2. clear　3. castle

尼斯湖水怪電影
A movie of the Loch Ness Monster

Now people come to Loch Ness with movie cameras and (1.　　　). They are going to make a movie. Nessie is going to be in the movies and (2.　　　). The monster is going to be a movie (3.　　　)! The men and women with the movie cameras wait beside the Loch or (4.　　　) the Loch in boats. Their movie cameras are (5.　　　). Their tape recorders are ready. But Nessie isn't ready.

The monster remains in deep water. People (6.　　　) movies, but does Nessie want them? We (7.　　　) television, but does the Loch Ness Monster like it?

＊第十六段測驗解答：

1. tape recorders　2. on television　3. star
4. go up and down　5. ready　6. want　7. like

CD＊17

電影明星 *Movie star*

The men and women with movie cameras say, "We cannot make our（1.　　　　）. We don't have our movie star."

They wait（2.　　　　）the Loch and wait and wait.

One man with a movie camera and a tape recorder is Tim Dinsdale. In（3.　　　　）he is watching beside Loch Ness.

"What's that over there?" he says one day. "Yes, it's the monster. It's Nessie." Soon, people are watching Tim Dinsdale's movie on television.　They can see a creature in the water, but what is it? It's not clear. Nessie is in a movie and on television, but the mystery remains.

＊第十七段測驗解答：

1. film　2. beside　3. 1960

這是尼斯湖水怪？
Is this the Loch Ness Monster?

"What is Nessie?" people ask.

Is the Loch Ness Monster a kind of （1.　　　　）?
Plesiosaurs don't live in our lakes today. They are
creatures from （2.　　　　）. But do they live in one or
two lakes （3.　　　　） in the water? Does a kind of
plesiosaur live in Loch Ness? Is Nessie a creature from
the past? That question is important.

Newspaper editors like the mystery of the Loch
Ness Monster story. But （4.　　　　） don't like
mysteries. They want （5.　　　　）.

＊第十八段測驗解答：

1. plesiosaur　2. the past　3. deep down

4. scientists　5. facts

監聽尼西 *Listen to Nessie*

The water of Loch Ness is not clear. Scientists cannot see in the deep water, but they can（1.　　　）. They put（2.　　　）tape recorders into the water and listen. The special tape recorders give facts to the scientists.

They listen and say, "Yes, Loch Ness has a big animal or fish in it."

"What is it? We don't know.　But a strange creature is there. That is（3.　　　）."

Scientists still listen with their special tape recorders in the water of Loch Ness. People still watch the Loch. They watch and wait.

Is the monster there too, deep in the water, watching and waiting?

＊第十段測驗解答：

1. listen　2. special　3. a fact

尼西生意 *Nessie in Business*

In Inverness you can buy Nessie. You can buy a picture of Nessie or a Loch Ness Monster （1.　　　）. You can buy a Loch Ness Monster （2.　　　）. You can （3.　　　） Nessie. You can have a Nessie in your （4.　　　）. The Loch Ness Monster is not only a mystery, it's （5.　　　）.

Visitors to Scotland always go to Loch Ness. They always see the Loch Ness Monster in the （6.　　　） of Inverness. The people of Inverness like Nessie. The monster is big business.

✳第二十段測驗解答：

1. book 2. game 3. wear 4. house
5. good business 6. shops

尼西到底是什麼？ *Nessie is?*

And that is the Loch Ness Monster — different （1.　　　　） to different people. Nessie is a monster or a dragon? It's a big fish or a plesiosaur — a creature from the past? Or it （2.　　　　） a creature? The photographs are only pictures of trees in the water.

Or boats?

Or （3.　　　　）?

No, the scientists tell us, "Nessie is real. A strange creature lives in the deep water of Loch Ness."

But （4.　　　　） is Nessie? （5.　　　　） is Nessie? Those questions （6.　　　　）.

That is the mystery of Loch Ness.

---

*第二十一段測驗解答：

1. things　2. isn't　3. birds　4. who　5. What　6. remain

知識性 故事性 趣味性的
英語有聲書

成寒英語有聲書 4
推理女神探
Level: 3

美國新英格蘭區的一座豪宅發生命案，被害人是男主人麥可‧葛瑞。警方派年輕貌美的女警探K前來調查。這是K負責偵辦的第一件案子，她發現屋子裡的人，包括女主人、女主人之弟、男主人舊日軍中同袍、年輕女祕書，還有女管家，每個人都有嫌疑，每個人都有犯罪的動機。可是K找不到任何犯案的證據，現場也找不到凶器，但男主人不是自殺的……這本推理小說，考你的判斷能力，究竟誰是凶手？這是一本德國、法國初中生必讀的英語課外讀本。全書彩色印刷，配上精采的插圖，CD多人情境化演出，句型簡單故事引人。台大醫學院教授張天鈞專文推薦。

躺著學英文2
青春‧英語‧向前行
Level: 6

所附的有聲書〈搭便車客〉，他從紐約啟程，沿著第66號公路往西行，目的地是加州。一路上，有個男子一直向他招手，想搭便車，他到底是誰？為何甩不掉他？不管車子開多快，他總是隨後跟來……音效逼真，一口氣聽到最後一秒，不聽到最後結局不甘心。

知識性　故事性　趣味性

躺著學英文3
打開英語的寬銀幕　Level: 5

所附的有聲書＜搭錯線＞，夜深人靜，一個行動不便的婦人獨自在家。她要接線生幫她接通老公辦公室的電話，不料搭錯線，她竟偷聽到兩個人在電話中談一件即將發生的謀殺案，就在今晚十一點一刻整，他們打算採取行動……CD的後半部特別加上中英有聲解說，打開讀者的耳朵，只要聽聽就會。政大英文系主任陳超明教授專文推薦。

成寒英語有聲書 1
綠野仙蹤　　　　　Level: 3

沒讀過美國經典作品《綠野仙蹤》，你可能看不懂、聽不懂許多英文，舞台劇的生動演出，節奏輕快，咬字清晰。讀者一致稱讚：英語有聲書很少是如此動聽的。中英文對照，附加生字、生詞解說及聽力測驗。採用大量插圖，圖文書編排。《成寒英語有聲書》是「正常速度」的英語，讓讀者一口氣聽下來，先享受聽故事的樂趣，再細讀文中的單字及片語的用法，學著開口說，然後試著寫。作家侯文詠專文推薦。

成寒英語有聲書 2
靈媒的故事
Level: 3

一個命運坎坷的棄兒，一出生就被丟在公車上。年少輕狂的他做小偷，終於被關入牢裡。在獄中他認識一個哈佛畢業的老頭子，這人看出棄兒天資聰穎，於是教他讀書，說一口漂亮的英語，還有做靈媒的各種技巧：預卜未來、知道過去，與亡者通靈。

孤兒從小偷一變成為靈媒，名聲遠播。許多人來求問前途，連警方都來找他幫忙破案……一則發人深省的故事。國家圖書館主任王岫專文推薦。

成寒英語有聲書 5
——一語動人心
Level: 5

如何讓你的演說或寫作更有力？那就是套用經典名句 (quotations)。從名人的文章和談話車，去學習這些句子的多重意義和各種用法。善用英語「經典名句」，在歡語寫作或演說時有加分的效果。本書收錄200多句經典名句，標準美語朗讀，配樂非常優美。這是一本可以陪你成長，隨時提升英語實力的有聲書。世新大學人文社會學院院長李振清專文推薦。

Studying系列⑰

成寒英語有聲書3——尼斯湖水怪之謎

編　著—成寒
副主編—莊瑞琳
美術編輯—高鶴倫、林麗華
企　畫—曾秉常
董事長—趙政岷
出版者—時報文化出版企業股份有限公司
　　　108019台北市和平西路三段二四〇號三樓
　　　發行專線—（〇二）二三〇六—六八四二
　　　讀者服務專線—〇八〇〇—二三一—七〇五·（〇二）二三〇四—七一〇三
　　　讀者服務傳真—（〇二）二三〇四—六八五八
　　　郵撥—一九三四四七二四時報文化出版公司
　　　信箱—10899台北華江橋郵局第九十九信箱
時報悅讀網—http://www.readingtimes.com.tw
電子郵件信箱—history@readingtimes.com.tw
法律顧問—理律法律事務所 陳長文律師、李念祖律師
印　刷—家佑實業股份有限公司
初版一刷—二〇〇四年一月十二日
二版一刷—二〇〇九年三月十日
二版十五刷—二〇二三年二月十三日
定　價—新台幣二〇〇元
版權所有　翻印必究（缺頁或破損的書，請寄回更換）

時報文化出版公司成立於一九七五年，並於一九九九年股票上櫃公開發行，於二〇〇八年脫離中時集團非屬旺中，以「尊重智慧與創意的文化事業」為信念。

ISBN 957-13-4036-7
Printed in Taiwan

成寒英語有聲書. 3, 尼斯湖水怪之謎 / 成寒編著.
—初版. — 臺北市 ：時報文化，2003 [民92]
面； 公分

ISBN 957-13-4036-7 （平裝附光碟片）

873.57   92022744